D0995189

THE
SCARECROW

THE
SCARECROW

Edgar J. Hyde

CCP

645983
MORAY COUNCIL
Department of Technical
& Leisure Services
JC

© 1998 Children's Choice Publications

Text supplied by Joseph Boyle

All rights reserved. No part of this publication may be reproduced, stored in a retrieval systemor transmitted, in any form or by any means, electronic, mechanical, photocopying, recording, or otherwise without the prior consent of the copyright holder.

ISBN 1-90201-209-7

Printed and bound in the UK

Contents

Chapter 1	7
Chapter 2	15
Chapter 3	23
Chapter 4	35
Chapter 5	43
Chapter 6	55
Chapter 7	65
Chapter 8	77
Chapter 9	87
Chapter 10	101
Epilogue	111

Chapter 1

"David, hurry up! Your breakfast is almost ready."

David rolled over in bed and groaned. School again. He loved that twilight zone between deep sleep and getting out of bed. He had been thinking about last weekend. His dad had taken him to the United game for the first time for ages. It was the league decider and United had won 2–0. What a game! A huge crowd, two great goals, and. . .

"David, get a move on!" Mrs Davies screamed at the top of her voice.

"I'm coming, I'm coming," David moaned, his mum's shrill voice disturbing his peace.

David jumped out of bed, paid a quick visit to the bathroom, and dressed hurriedly. He looked round his room for the shoes discarded the night before. His room was covered in the usual adolescent mess of clothing, sports gear, and old magazines.

After a few minutes he appeared in the downstairs hallway, dressed in what could loosely be described as the school uniform. Well, he had the school tie on at least. The rest looked as if it had been contributed by a rap group. Baggy shirt, baggy jumper, and baggy trousers. Thank God baggy was still in.

David's two sisters were already half way through their bowls of cornflakes or muesli or whatever healthy concoction they were into these days. In David's opinion having two older sisters was the worst bad joke God could have played on a boy. David had just turned 13, Sarah was 14 (and a half, as she liked to remind everyone) and Emma was almost 16.

Between their fascination with clothes, make-up and all-boy bands, David felt, at times, as though life was almost unbearable.

"David, the school bus is going to be here in 15 minutes and look at the state of you!" Mum said with a sigh.

"OK Mum, don't panic. Where's Dad?" David quizzed, peering out of the kitchen window.

"He is over in the far field checking on some of the sheep. He thinks that fox has been about again. The chickens were making an awful racket last night. He'll be back in a minute," replied Mrs Davies, throwing some toast on to David's plate.

David's dad was a farmer and the family had just recently moved to the area. The new farm was absolutely massive and was at least three times the size of the farm they had lived on before. Not only had they more sheep and cattle, but they had twice as much land.

The only problem was that David's dad had so much work to do that he had very little time to spend with his son. With only two sisters for company, on an isolated farm, David could be a handful at times. Boredom easily set in, and he was always getting into trouble for some of his antics. His imagination and his bad taste in practical jokes were always the cause of friction between he and his sisters. Sarah, he could just about tolerate, but Emma he had no time for at all. He thought she was on another planet.

"Well Emma, meeting Steve at lunchtime today again?" David asked, smirking at his oldest sister.

"Mum, tell him to mind his own business. I refuse to talk to him after Friday's performance. He is a complete embarrassment." Emma pouted, turning away.

Emma was referring to the teasing or, more accurately abuse, David and his friends had subjected Emma and her 'latest' to, when he had spotted them walking hand in hand on the way to class. A fair target in David's mind – although he had been forced to make a fast exit when the almost six-foot Steve had decided he had taken enough and went after his new love's younger brother.

"Emma, don't give me any hassle," David whispered, "or I'll tell them what I saw you up to on Wednesday, and that didn't look like Steve to me, although his face was difficult to see, with yours all over it!"

"You're a pig!!" Emma snapped, storming off to her room. Sarah followed, scowling at her brother as only sisters know how to.

"David, give it a rest will you. I'm fed up

with all this bickering!" barked David's mum. "Eat your breakfast."

David looked out of the window again. His dad had just climbed over the fence next to the large barn where they stored most of the winter hay. The barn was also home to the family's hens. He was carrying the double-barrelled shotgun he usually took out to scare off unwanted visitors. Foxes and crows were the usual targets. David opened the kitchen door and ran out to meet his dad.

"Hey Dad, everything alright?" David asked. "Any problem with the sheep?"

"Nope, everything seems OK," Mr Davies replied. "That fox must have gone to ground. Those chickens woke me up again last night. What a noise. Just wait till we fetch that new dog next week. That'll put the frighteners up him alright."

David's old family dog had disappeared two weeks previously. Nobody knew what had happened to him. David's dad had guessed he had got stuck down some old fox hole and not managed to get out. He had been a good dog for making sure the local foxes had been kept at bay. But now he was no more! It had upset David, especially, at the time. The dog was often David's only companion on the farm and they had spent a lot of time together.

"Do me a favour Davy, son, will you," Mr Davies shouted as he kicked off his boots outside the kitchen door. "Go and fetch me half a dozen eggs from the barn, I could do with a couple of nice fresh boiled eggs, I'm famished."

"Sure, Dad," David replied, running off to the barn, pleased to help his dad, and disappearing inside

"Morning girls, where's my tea?" Mr Davies demanded jokingly as he opened the kitchen door.

"Where it usually is, in the pot, help yourself," Mum replied tidying up the girls' dishes "I hope you took off those dirty boots."

They were all stopped in their tracks with a sudden, chilling scream from the barn.

"Ddd—aa—dd, Ddd—aa—dd! Help! Help!"

"Oh my God, John, that's David! What's happened? What's happened?"

Chapter 2

Mr Davies burst out of the kitchen door and crossed the yard in a flash. He ran into the barn, his eyes darting all over, searching for his son. Apart from the barn entrance, the barn was in darkness, the early morning sunshine not yet penetrating the barn's broad span.

"David, where are you, are you alright?" Mr Davies stammered, his eyes trying to peer through the darkness, as they adjusted from the bright sunshine of the courtyard.

"Dd—aa—dd, Ddd—aa—dd!"

The big farmer caught sight of his son standing in the far right hand corner of the barn. He rushed to his side.

"David, are you OK? What's going on?" Mr Davies asked worriedly.

David appeared to be uninjured. He was standing poker straight, his mouth open with his lower jaw almost on his chest. His eyes were glazed and fixed straight ahead. David's dad scanned his son from head to toe, running his hands up and down his son's body.

"What happened to you? Did you fall? Have you hurt yourself?" His dad asked, his voice becoming less frantic as he could see no obvious injury.

But still David stared ahead, his eyes fixed as if in deep shock. Eventually David turned his gaze towards his dad's face. His dad looked into his son's eyes and then followed his eyes as David once again turned his head to look straight ahead. At the same time David raised his arm, his finger pointing to a figure about four yards from where they stood. There was no need for David to point now, his dad could see what was holding his son's stare so strongly.

Four yards away lying back on pile of hay was a dark shape. At first the shape was difficult to make out. However, quickly it became unmistakable. It was a body. A man's body. Mr Davies feared the worst. But this body was not still and this body's eyes were not closed. The man was alive. David's dad could clearly see the body shaking all over, as if connected to some constant electrical charge, and the white of it's two eyes sharply pierced the dimness of the barn.

"Go into the house, David – tell your mum you're alright," Dad whispered, pushing David away with his broad hand and staring at the mysterious and unwelcome figure.

There was no need. David's mum had followed her husband across the yard and the sound of her arrival at the barn entrance seemed to inject more electrical charge into the shaking figure and cause the already wide white eyes to open wider.

"Stay back, Karen. David, you too. See to your mum, son."

But David was still too shocked to move. He watched as his father edged closer to the trembling figure. Mr Davies reached out his hand and laid it firmly on the man's shoulder.

"Who the devil are you, man? What's happened to you? What are you doing here?" Dad's voice trembled, betraying the nervousness they all felt.

Dad's approach and contact only seemed to send another 200 volts into the already shock-ridden body. To everyone's surprise the man jumped up and in one movement, threw the big farmer to the floor and started for the barn entrance. David's dad was a big man and it seemed unlikely that he could so easily be pushed down by a man who looked no more than half his size. The sudden movement seemed to shake David from his trance. Seeing his dad thumped to the floor, David threw himself at the man's feet, sending him hurtling into the numerous hen coops that housed the family's army of hens. Amongst the flapping wings and tangled chicken wire, the man struggled to get to his feet. There was no point. David's dad was now back on his feet and no longer in any mood to hold back on this unwelcome visitor. Any concern or sympathy he had previously felt, had now gone. Mr Davies's size 12 foot buried itself deep in the man's stomach. Once, twice, and then a third time, followed swiftly by a right hook full square on his jaw. The man slumped to the floor semi-conscious.

"David, go with your mum. 'Phone the police. They'll have to attend to this one, now. I'll entertain him here till they get here," Mr Davies instructed, his voice now full of his usual composure.

David ran over to his mum and the two quickly made for the house, keen to call for help.

"Well then, stranger. What do you have to say for yourself?" Mr Davies questioned, lifting the man to his feet and sitting him down on top of one of the overturned chicken coops.

The man's body had stopped shaking, but his eyes were as wide as ever, displaying what now in clearer light seemed like sheer terror.

"Come on now, speak up," the farmer insisted.

The man looked hard into Mr Davies's eyes, his own eyes seeming to search the big farmer's for help.

"Well? What are you doing here? Tell me, man. Do you want another thump?" Mr

Chapter 2

Davies shouted, losing patience. He grabbed and shook the man's shoulder, frustrated by the lack of response.

The man opened his mouth, a trickle of blood appearing at the corner of lips. He seemed to mutter something but it was no more than a garble, and barely audible.

"What? What are you trying to say? Speak up. Speak up man," insisted Mr Davies.

Again the stranger started to open his mouth, and again no sense could be made of the noises made. His two hands went to his mouth, as if trying to prise out the words he seemed unable to utter. The noises he was making were no more than moans and groans. He then crumbled to the floor with noises that, this time, were unmistakable. The man was sobbing uncontrollably. Mr Davies looked down bemused at the pathetic figure before him.

"Well, you'll talk soon enough when

you're behind bars. You had better have something to say for yourself then," Mr Davies snapped, offering no pity to the stranger.

Chapter 3

Three days had passed since the episode in the barn. The police had seemed to take forever to show up. Mr Davies had been unable to get any sense out of the strange visitor.

When the police eventually did appear, the stranger was no longer a stranger. He was well known to them. His name apparently was John Morrison, a well-known local thief, somebody who was very familiar with the inside of police cells. He had a police record as long as his arm

According to the police, he had been a real 'hard nut' in his time, and the sight of him broken down and sobbing, the way he had been that day, had really puzzled them. Morrison was not easily intimated or frightened by anyone.

He had still not said an intelligible word up to the time he was thrown, wailing, into the back of the police car.

David was in his room, still a little shaken from his recent experience, wondering about it all, when he heard the doorbell ring. He hadn't seen or heard the police car approach as he was lost in his own world, imagining all the possible causes that had brought that strange man to their barn in that state.

"David! Will you get that son? My hands are covered at the moment," Mrs Davies shouted from outside the kitchen backdoor.

David's mum had been cleaning out the mess in the chicken coops in the barn. So

God knows what her hands were covered in.

David ran down the stairs. The shape through the glass of the front door was unmistakable. One of Her Majesty's constabulary was calling. Either that, or his dad had grown a large boil on top of his head.

David opened the door.

"Morning son. Is your dad in?" Constable Collins enquired, looking beyond David into the hallway.

It took about fifteen minutes for David to retrieve his dad from his tractor in one of the fields close by. He was still angry with the intruder who had upset his family and he wanted no more to do with it. The policeman's visit only disturbed his busy day.

In the meantime, David's mum, hands suitably cleansed, had fed and watered the patient constable. In the fifteen minutes wait he had remained straight-faced, full of serious intent, and unwilling to give any hint of the purpose of his visit.

Eventually everyone had gathered in the front room. Emma and Sarah had come down from their rooms. There was no way that they were going to miss the excitement. It wasn't every day that their house was the centre of police activity. Although Emma seemed more interested in admiring the polished constable's blue eyes as a match for his blue uniform. David looked at his sisters and shook his head in mock disgust.

Constable Collins stood up and walked to the window. He seemed a little reluctant to talk. After a few seconds he turned around and started.

"I am afraid I have some disturbing news." He paused. "Perhaps you would prefer the children to leave the room, Mr Davies?" the constable suggested, looking first at David and then the girls.

"No it's fine, officer, go ahead. They are

all big enough and ugly enough now," he replied.

"Very well, sir. I am sorry to tell you that the man we apprehended here the other day, one John Morrison, is now dead." The constable hesitated. He looked at the faces round the room. It wasn't as if some close relative had died, but the constable's words stunned them. It was a mixture of shock and puzzlement. The image of the man trembling in the barn and then being escorted away by the police was still fresh in all their minds. And now he was dead.

"What happened?" Mr Davies asked a little tentatively.

The officer continued.

"After we left here the other day Morrison was taken to the James Street Police Station. All the way, during the journey it was impossible to make any sense of what he was trying to say. I had met Morrison before, two or three times, and he was a clever chap. Crooked, yes, but sharp and witty. He was always full of banter. I couldn't believe this was the same man in the car with us that night. It was clear something very significant had happened to him. His inability to speak sensibly, together with the mixture of fear and pain we could sense in his face and motions, disturbed us greatly."

David looked round the room. His sisters' silly grins had disappeared and his mother's face looked ashen. His dad's face was expressionless.

"As soon as we booked him into the station we called in the police doctor on duty. He was only in the man's cell a minute or two when he shouted us in to ask who the man was and if any of us had spoken to him recently. I confirmed that I knew him and had spoken to him several times in the past.

I told him it had been about a month since we had arrested him last on suspicion of a local robbery and that he was very vocal then – we couldn't shut him up. He complained constantly of being harassed.

"Well," the doctor said, "He certainly can't talk now, and he never will talk again. This man has no tongue. He has had it ripped from his mouth."

At this the policeman stopped in his tracks. He obviously was still affected by the details of his story. But there was more to come.

The room was deadly silent now, and the faces and expressions were becoming even more puzzled.

"Good God, what happened? His tongue? But how did he die?" Dad asked, his voice a mixture of shock and amazement.

"Please wait sir, let me continue," the officer interrupted.

"All of us at the station were stunned too. But the concern for Morrison didn't stop there. The man was ranting and raving like a lunatic, unable to speak, but making plenty of noise. He was jumping around, his eyes staring like a mad dog. He was in real danger of doing himself further injury. The doctor quickly insisted that he be taken to St. Gerard's asylum where he could be properly evaluated. He was transferred immediately. I accompanied him myself in the transfer to the asylum and I was there when they locked him in the asylum cell. They had just given him a strong sedative and thankfully at last he was beginning to calm down. I was feeling very relieved to be able to go home. Morrison's injuries and behaviour were really disturbing me. I had never seen anything like it.

"The next morning, I turned up at the station at the usual time. But as soon as I entered the office, I could tell that something was wrong. There was a real atmosphere about the place. I had just reached my desk when Sergeant Grant called for me to go into his office.

"Collins," he said, his face as stern as I had ever seen it. "Morrison's dead. Hung himself in his cell, some time during the night. The doctor's just been here. He's already been up to the asylum and seen to the body. Strange business. What on earth happened to the man?"

I couldn't believe what I was hearing. The whole episode was becoming more absurd. I couldn't understand what could possibly have caused Morrison such injury and drive him to such drastic action.

The sergeant wasn't finished however. A crumpled piece of A4 paper lay in the middle of his desk. He pushed it towards me.

"Have a look at that. They found this in Morrison's cell. It looks like his writing."

At that, the constable stopped and put his hand into his jacket pocket and pulled out a crumpled piece of paper.

"This is the note. It's completely ridiculous, but the Sergeant asked me to show it to you and see if it would mean anything to you. Seeing as he was found on your property."

The constable leaned over and passed the paper to Mr Davies. David, and the two girls all ran round behind his chair. Only Mrs Davies remained where she was. Mr Davies smoothed out the paper and held it out in front of him. The writing was messy but the words were clear enough. It read:

God help me. God help us all. I beg you to believe me. I am so scared, but I am not mad. I have never been so scared in all my life. I can't stand it. My tongue has gone, ripped out by a wooden monster, a monster come to life in front of my very eyes. He will find me here. He will come for me. I begged him to spare me, I was only going to take a few things – a radio, some money, no big deal. But this wooden monster, this scarecrow would not let me go. You must stop him. Stop him. I beg you. God save my soul—

Mr Davies stood up, thrusting the note back into the policeman's hand.

"What is this nonsense? The man obviously was mad. Wooden monster? Scarecrow? This whole thing is just ridiculous."

The constable moved towards the sitting room door.

"So I take it this all means nothing to you too?" he asked. "We had to ask, in case any of it made any sense to you."

"Of course it doesn't make any sense," Mr Davies snapped angrily. "This madman has come onto our land, upset my family, and now he has killed himself. This is the last I want to hear of all this."

"Well thank you, anyway," Constable Collins said starting to make for the hallway. "I am sorry to have disturbed you. The whole episode is disturbing for us all. We don't get much of this sort of thing here."

Constable Collins went out to his car and drove off. Mr Davies made off, shaking his head, heading to where he left his tractor. Mrs Davies went to the kitchen and put the kettle on. She needed a cup of tea. The two girls ran upstairs, upset by the story they had heard below. Only David remained in the room. He sat motionless staring out of the sitting room window. His eyes seemed fixed on something. If you had followed his gaze, you would have seen the distant figure in the far field. The old farm scarecrow.

Chapter 4

David stared out of the window. He couldn't take his eyes off the scarecrow in the field next to the house. The scarecrow stood in an uncultivated field next to the house. It was a field that his father still hadn't had time to work on. It had always seemed strange to David that the only scarecrow on the farm stood in a field that didn't need one. His dad had continually said that he was going to move it. But like many other jobs on the farm, it just hadn't been done.

David was confused and he was becoming a little scared. As he stared at the erect figure in the field he began to think of his old dog. He had been satisfied with his dad's version of the dog's disappearance. After all, the daft old dog had been constantly chasing foxes, and getting stuck down fox holes was the regular demise of over-zealous hounds. However he had never mentioned to anyone, especially his dad, the other version that had been suggested for the dog's absence.

Two days after the dog had gone missing, David had been standing on the road outside the farm waiting for the school bus. He was upset. His dog had never disappeared before. His dad had told him that he would probably never see his old friend again. His sisters, as usual, were late and hadn't come out yet. An old man had appeared suddenly at his side. The smell of alcohol announcing his arrival as much as anything. He had been sleeping under a nearby hedge. 'Old Jonesy' was a well known local celebrity. He was a down-and-out drunk, rarely sober enough to recognise whether it was night or day. However he could often bring a smile to your face with his quick wit and his many stories.

"Now then, young Davy, how are you. What's wrong. Why so glum?" Jonesy had asked, noticing the boy's concerned face.

"We've not seen Sandy, our dog since yesterday evening. He's disappeared," David had replied. Jonesy's grin left his face, replaced with a deep frown.

"Ah, well son, you'll not see him again. He's gone for sure. Gone for ever," the old man mumbled.

"Gone, what do you mean?" David had pressed, a little agitated.

The old man put his arm around David. The smell of stale alcohol was overpowering.

He continued, "He's ran off. I saw him

with my own eyes. Chased off by that wooden thing. That scarecrow over there." The old man jerked his head in the direction of the farm. He continued. "Chased him all the way over the fields. The daft animal was howling like a banshee. No, you'll not see him again."

David had laughed at the time. The thought of the scarecrow running across his dad's fields chasing after his old dog was the sort of crazy story old Jonesy was famous for.

But, as David recalled the encounter with the old man, now he was not laughing. In fact he was beginning to feel more and more scared. Morrison's note had talked about a wooden monster, a scarecrow. Was it a coincidence? Just nonsense spoken by two madmen? He couldn't tell his dad about Old Jonesy's story. He would just laugh at him. But now, after reading Morrison's note it was all becoming a bit weird.

David decided he had to find Old Jonesy again. He had to talk to him again about what the old man had seen that night. David stared out the window, one last time, peered at the wooden shape in the field and shook his head.

David ran to the hut at the side of the house, pulled out his bike and made off as fast as he could towards town. It usually took David about twenty minutes to cycle into town, but this time the journey seemed over in less than half of that. Jonesy had a number of usual hang-outs in town during the day. He would normally be trying to make some money pleading poverty, or alternatively spending money on his staple diet of cheap wine.

It didn't take David long to catch sight of the sad old figure. He was propped up at the corner of one of the town's two pubs, held upright by a combination of the side of the building and a large overflowing dustbin. David quickly cycled over and shouted to the old man. The old man didn't respond. David climbed off his bike and walked slowly to the corner of the pub. Still the old man's head was down, slumped on his chest.

"Jonesy, it's me Davy, I have to talk to you," David said approaching the old man.

"Jonesy, are you OK? It's me Davy," he added, becoming a little agitated by the old man's lack of response.

Finally, the old man raised his head. David was instantly shocked. The old man looked into his eyes. David immediately recognised the look in the old man's eyes. It was that same frightened fixed stare that he had seen on Morrison's face in the barn. David hesitated, almost too scared to speak.

"Jonesy, what's happened? Are you OK?" David asked, taking the old man's arm.

The old man started to shake his head. David spotted tears welling up in his eyes.

Chapter 4

The old man started to open his mouth. David spotted for the first time the dried blood clinging to the old man's beard. As the old man opened his mouth wider, David gasped and staggered back, the power in his legs disappearing rapidly.

Jonesy's tongue was gone.

Chapter 5

If the journey to town had been pretty fast, the journey back was even faster. David had thrown his bike into the hut and sprinted through the house, up the stairs and into his room, slamming the door hard.

His mind was totally confused, a mixture of puzzlement and fear. But what was he to do? Who could he talk to? He was pretty convinced now that there was real danger close by. Two men connected with his house had both had their tongues ripped out, and his dog's disappearance seemed connected. Even if it had nothing to do with a scarecrow coming to life, there was something going on that had frightened these two men so badly, left one speechless and one dead.

David sat through dinner in silence, barely touching his food. His mind preoccupied with the scarecrow. He still hadn't said anything to anyone.

"Well at least we can all have a lie in tomorrow," said Mrs Davies, putting the kettle on for the umpteenth time that day.

"Thank God for that. That rooster was beginning to drive me crazy," added Mr Davies.

David looked up, not quite taking in the significance of the conversation.

"Well someone had better go and get rid of it before it starts smelling the place," Mrs Davies insisted.

"Honey, this is a farm. One more bad smell is hardly going to make a difference,"

Mr Davies replied with a broad grin on his face. "I'll sort it out later." He added quickly, seeing the scowl appearing on his wife's face.

David started to pay attention. "What are you talking about?" he asked. "What's going on?"

Sarah chipped in, "David, where has your head been all day? Sometimes you don't have a clue!"

"Dad, found the rooster dead this morning son, round at the side of the barn. The old thing must have just been too old. Probably fell off the top of the barn. Either that or your dad threw his boot at it at half-past five this morning, Mrs Davies explained.

"Where is it now?" David asked, standing up.

"Same place. Don't worry I'll sort it out after my tea," Mr Davies said, seeing something of concern in his son's face.

But it was more than concern.

David had to see the bird. He had to check something out. He immediately ran out of the kitchen and across to the barn.

"What's got into him all of a sudden?" Mr Davies quizzed. "He hated the noise the damn thing made every morning too."

David turned the corner of the barn and immediately saw the dead bird lying on top of an old farm fence. David looked up to the top of the barn. The bird was lying directly under the spot in the roof where he could be found every morning at sunrise. Well, where he used to be found.

"Maybe Mum was right," David thought, "it probably fell off the roof."

But the more David thought about it, the more he knew it didn't sound right. Birds don't fall off roofs. David looked to his left, less than twenty yards away stood the figure that was becoming more and more sinister, the scarecrow. There it stood, still and erect. Harmless looking enough, but intimidating all the same. David looked again at the dead rooster lying in front of him.

David stepped forward and leaned down. He picked up a stick and prodded the bird. It was dead alright. The rooster's head was hidden underneath its body. David used the stick to prise the head out. He flicked the stick and the whole bird rolled over. The head was clear now. The head and neck lay limp, the way David had seen many times when his Dad had decided it was going to be chicken for Sunday dinner. His Dad had shown David how to kill a chicken by wringing its neck and had even suggested he try it. David had always declined. He thought it looked so cruel. This rooster looked as if it had died the same way. Its head and neck were contorted and twisted. There was only one more thing to do. David had to look inside the bird's mouth. He had to know if this incident could be added to all the other goings-on.

David dropped the stick and kneeled on the ground. With one hand he took hold of the bird by the neck and lifted it up. With his other hand he prised open its beak. David knew what to expect this time. There was no shock, but there was fear. The rooster's tiny tongue had gone.

"David, what on earth are you doing? Put that thing down," Mr Davies shouted as he turned the barn corner.

David was still kneeling on the ground, with the bird by the neck. He threw it to the ground.

"What's got into you, David? That thing is stinking," added Mr Davies.

David stood up, frightened and confused. Mr Davies could see there was something wrong.

"What is it, David? You look as if you have seen a ghost. It was only an old rooster. The thing was a damn nuisance. I'm glad to see the back of it," Mr Davies said, picking the bird up and throwing it into a black bag he had brought from the kitchen.

David couldn't get any words out. He wanted to tell his dad that this was the third time, today alone, he had seen or heard about somebody or something having its tongue ripped out. But Mr Davies had already dismissed Morrison's note as the work of a madman. He certainly wouldn't take old Jonesy seriously, and a dead rooster was not going to convince him much either. David couldn't say anything yet.

But he was so scared, he had to do something. He felt there was real danger on the farm.

Mr Davies disappeared round the back of the barn, where most of the farm refuse was dumped, carrying the dead rooster. David looked again at the wooden figure in the field. He was really frightened now, but he had to do it. He had to have a close look at the scarecrow.

David waited by the barn until he heard the noise of his dad returning to the kitchen. He heard the door close. It was beginning to get dark now and the kitchen lights were beginning to spread across the duskiness of the courtyard.

David approached the wooden fence separating the courtyard from the overgrown field. He looked back towards the kitchen. He could clearly see his mum in the kitchen tidying up. His dad was sitting at the table. Somehow David felt a little bit less frightened, more secure, knowing they were close by. He climbed over the fence.

The grass and weeds in the field stretched up to David's knees. As David struggled to put one foot in front of the other, he wondered again why his dad still hadn't worked on this field. His mum had certainly nagged him enough about it. She had continually said that she was fed up looking out of her kitchen window at the overgrown land in front of her.

David looked up. The darkening figure was now only a few yards away. David inhaled deeply, as if trying to hold his breath as he approached. Finally he was there. David let out a long gasp of air, almost in relief, trying to calm his nerves. He didn't know what he had expected to see, but as he scanned the wooden man in front of him, he could see nothing, for the moment, that was out of the ordinary.

David was no expert on scarecrows, but this one looked like all the others he had seen in farms around. It looked like a regular farm scarecrow. Wooden head, brush handle arms, old suit, hat, and plenty of straw. Loads of straw. In fact for such an old scarecrow that nobody had paid any attention to, or looked after, it was in remarkably good condition. It didn't look years old, as it must have been. The old lady that sold them the farm had briefly mentioned the scarecrow, saying that it had been there when she bought the farm twenty years earlier.

David was beginning to feel better. The incidents of the last few days were beginning to disappear in his mind as he looked at this unremarkable figure in front of him. David reached out to straighten the scarecrow's hat. He must have been a little nervous still, as his fingers twitched and the hat went tumbling to the ground. David leaned down and picked the hat up. He was just about to replace it on top of the bald wooden head, when he noticed that there was some writing engraved into the top of the scarecrow's head. David stood on his toes as he tried to make out the writing. He struggled to get high enough to read the words clearly.

He looked around. It was getting very dark now. He could just make out the outline of a small pile of bricks a couple of yards away. David hurriedly lifted two or three bricks to the side of the scarecrow, putting one on top of the other. He stood up on the top brick. Standing a little shakily and holding on to the stretched out arm of the scarecrow, David could now see the words etched on the scarecrow's head. David read silently and slowly to himself.

> This land is yours for you to scare
> All beings who perchance do
>   dare
> To disturb or threaten without
>   pity
> This house's peace and prosper-
>   ity.

David's feet slipped from the top brick and he fell to the ground in a heap. He got to the fence in a second and he leapt it in one movement. He ran as fast as his feet would carry him towards the safety of the kitchen light.

Chapter 6

David's sister Sarah sat alone in the kitchen. The rest of the family had moved through to the sitting room. David had to say something to somebody now. He could no longer keep all that he knew and had seen to himself. He was still too afraid to talk to his dad.

As David burst through the kitchen door, Sarah didn't even look up from her magazine. She was well used to her brother scampering all over the house, dashing here and there in a constant hurry. David was a walking noise machine.

"Sarah," David started, his voice lowered in an attempt to ensure no-one in the next room heard what he was about to say.

Sarah didn't lift her eyes from her magazine, but answered, "What?"

"Sarah, listen to me. I have something really important to tell you," David continued.

Sarah looked at her brother now. She had sensed something different in her brother's voice. As she looked at him she could see the worry on his face.

"What is it, David? You look terrible. Where have you been? I hope you haven't been messing about with that dead rooster." Sarah said wondering what was bothering her brother.

"Sarah, listen to me. I am going to tell you something amazing. You have to believe what I am going to tell you. I need to tell someone before I go crazy."

David related all the recent events. Sarah

obviously knew the details about Morrison but he explained to her about his two encounters with Jonesy. When David reached the part of his story where he discovered that Jonesy had also lost his tongue, Sarah stood up.

"David, stop it you're scaring me," she snapped.

"Sssshhh, Sarah. I know," David went on. "I'm scared too, but I have to tell you. Please, just listen."

Sarah sat down. David told her about the rooster and the words written on the scarecrow's head. He couldn't remember the words exactly, but he could remember their message. This scarecrow was supposed to scare off anybody who threatened the farm.

"David, are you at it again? This isn't funny. If you are at it, I am going to tell Dad this time," Sarah demanded, not knowing whether to believe her brother or not. Certainly Sarah could see that her brother appeared to be seriously upset. But her brother had proved before that he could be as good an actor as anyone.

"Sarah. This is all true, honestly. You have to believe me," pleaded David.

"David, do you realise what you are suggesting? Do you realise what all this will mean, if its true?" Sarah asked nervously. "If this is true, it means our scarecrow is running round the local countryside, scaring and maiming anyone who comes near our farm."

"Only those who threaten it," added David, going over the words in his mind.

"But why the tongues. What's the point of ripping out the tongues?" Sarah asked.

"I'm not sure," replied David. "Perhaps, with people, it's to try to stop them explaining what they had seen."

"Maybe," Sarah continued, "but what about the animals, the dog and the rooster.

Why harm them?"

David thought for a moment. He tried to remember the words on the scarecrow's head.

"I think the words said something about threatening the farm's peace. Sandy was forever barking, especially at night, and that rooster made a hell of a noise. Perhaps the scarecrow saw them as threatening the farm's peace. We brought them with us from the old farm. So maybe he thought he had to scare them off too," suggested David.

He really was confused now. But he was more sure than ever that the farm scarecrow had something to do with Morrison, old Jonesy, his dog, and the dead rooster. The words on the scarecrow's head were the final confirmation.

Sarah moved over to the kitchen window. The image of the scarecrow was growing in her mind. She strained her eyes trying to make out the figure in the field through the evening darkness.

Sarah spoke nervously "David," her voice began to tremble, "David, come here, look."

David joined her at the window. He looked out.

"Oh my God!" he said under his breath. "Oh, no!"

David ran to the kitchen door, he sped across the courtyard to the fence. His sister stayed a few paces behind. The two of them stared into the field. The empty field. The scarecrow had gone.

The spot where David had been only ten minutes before was clear except for the small pile of bricks.

"What do we do now, David? I'm really scared," Sarah asked, almost in tears.

David stared out into the empty field. He had to tell his dad now. Surely when he saw the empty field, he too would believe the scarecrow was at the root of all the strange happenings of the last few days.

David took his sister's arm and led her back to the kitchen. As they were entering the kitchen they could hear someone coming through from the sitting room.

"Hi, kids, what are you two up to?" Mr Davies asked, throwing his newspaper into the bin. "The game's starting in a minute on TV, David."

David didn't know where to start. He looked at Sarah's worried face. He had to tell him. "Dad," he stammered, "the scarecrow. . ." he hesitated as he could see the expression on his dad's face change. He knew his dad would take some convincing. But the missing scarecrow now would be the evidence David needed to get his dad to piece all the events together, as he had done.

"Dad, look at the scarecrow," David continued nervously. Mr Davies was already standing at the kitchen sink. He had just started to clean some dishes.

"Now, David I don't want to hear any more of this scarecrow business. That guy the other night was just a nutcase," Mr Davies snapped.

"Dad, please, just look.," David cried pleadingly.

"OK, OK, I'm looking, so what?" Replied Mr Davies puzzled.

"Dad, can't you see? Where's the scarecrow?" David added, almost pleading with his father to acknowledge what he and his sister had just witnessed.

"David, what are you on about? It's right there, where it normally is. What's got into you today?" Mr Davies replied, putting the tea-towel in his hand over the chair and heading back to the sitting room.

David went over to the window and looked out. Sarah joined him. They both looked out again into the darkness, to the field they had been to only a few minutes previously.

The scarecrow was there, standing erect and still in its usual position.

Chapter 7

David woke up very tired the next morning. He had hardly slept at all during the night. After he had seen the scarecrow back in his usual position, David had been unable to tell his dad any more about his theory of what their farm scarecrow was up to. Sarah and he had gone to his room and talked for hours, trying to make some sense of it all. Even after his mum had sent them all to bed, Sarah had come back in.

As he climbed out of bed, David wondered for a second if it had all been a dream. He wished it were all a dream. He pulled the window curtain back and looked at the figure in the field.

"Who are you? What are you?" David thought, the sense of fear beginning to rise in him again. The brief sleep that he had managed had been a welcome respite from the constant feeling of fear in his head and stomach that had been with him all the previous day

As he headed for the bathroom, Sarah was coming up the stairs. His sister's worried face confirmed that it had been no dream. They were living a nightmare.

David knew he had to tell his dad. He had decided he would try again that evening. He would write it all down during the day, while he was at school, getting it all clear in his own mind, and try to convince him that they had witnessed the scarecrow there one minute, gone the next, only to reappear again. Scarecrows aren't supposed to do that. At least Sarah had been there, she had witnessed the scarecrow's vanishing act.

They had agreed to not mention anything till they got home from school later. They would then get their dad in the sitting room and explain it all.

David washed and dressed slowly. As he came down the stairs, he could hear his parents' voices clearly in the kitchen. Sarah and Emma were still in their rooms, so his mum and dad were alone in the kitchen. David hesitated, their voices were becoming stronger. They were arguing. They rarely argued. Both of his parents were fairly easygoing people and Mr Davies usually went well out of his way to make sure that nothing upset his wife. David wondered what was the problem. He silently carried on down the stairs. He stopped on the bottom step and listened.

"But this is serious this time, John," Mrs

Davies said anxiously, "what are we going to do?"

"Listen Karen, don't worry. We have had money problems before and we have always come through. We'll sort this one out too," replied Mr Davies trying to calm his wife.

"Yes, but how? How do we find the money this time? You said you had been to all the banks and it was no good. They were not prepared to help. What's left to do? We are going to lose it all," Mrs Davies continued. David could sense his mum was now crying.

"Don't upset yourself, Karen. We'll work it out," replied Mr Davies. "Mr Kerr, the manager is coming round this evening. I am sure he will try to help us. He was the one who agreed to the mortgage on the farm in the first place, so he's bound to want to help."

"But he's the man who has written this letter. He's the one who is bringing the whole matter to a head. John, you will have to come up with something else," Mrs Davies insisted, her voice trembling.

"We'll see tonight. I'll know better after I have had a talk with Mr Kerr. Don't worry, pet. Come on, the children will be down in a minute. Don't let them see you're upset. We don't want to worry them," said Mr Davies

David slowly went back upstairs. He didn't want to see his mum crying. His sisters were still in their rooms. He could hear Emma singing along to some CD she had bought the day before and Sarah was obviously drying her hair, the noise of the dryer competing with the music.

David collected his school bag, making sure he had everything. He had forgotten for the time being about the scarecrow. The conversation downstairs was bothering him now. He knew his dad had borrowed a lot of money to buy the farm. He had explained that to them all when he warned them that there would be no big holidays for a year or two – not until he could get the first couple of harvests in. Something must have happened. David looked out of the window. He caught sight of the scarecrow again.

"Now we have two big problems," he thought.

The day passed slowly at school. David found it impossible to concentrate. His teacher had shouted at him a few times, chiding him for staring into space. David had considered telling his teacher, but he didn't know her well yet. He had wished he had been back at his old school. Mr Cairns, his old teacher, would have listened to his story about the scarecrow. He would have known what to do.

David had seen Sarah at lunchtime. Her teacher had almost sent her home. Her face was so white, and she had been physically sick at break time. But Sarah was keen to spend as much time away from the farm as she could. Away from the scarecrow.

David was relieved when the last bell went. He had been preparing himself all day. Trying to work out how best to tell his dad about the scarecrow. But now there was this money business. It was going to be hard to get his dad's attention.

David sat beside Sarah on the bus home. But they didn't say a word. Emma had gone straight to a friend's house to stay over. The two of them stepped off the bus and slowly walked up the path to the farmhouse. David couldn't resist looking over to the field. Sarah stared at the ground. She didn't lift her eyes until they had entered the house.

"Hi kids, we're going to have an early dinner tonight. Dad's got a visitor coming," Mrs Davies announced as they entered the kitchen. "Go and do your homework straight away. It'll be ready in about 45 minutes," she added.

David and Sarah went off up to their rooms. David decided it would probably be better to talk to his dad after he had met the bank manager. If David had understood what this morning's conversation between his parents was about he was sure that his dad was be in no mood right then to listen to his son's crazy story. He was sure his dad would sort everything out and would be in a better mood later.

Mr Davies was in the room that he used as a sort of study, next to the sitting room. He kept all his paperwork there. There was a lot of paperwork in the running of a farm. He sat at his desk, going through the numbers over and over again. He knew he was in real trouble this time. He had borrowed a lot of money to buy the farm and he had agreed specific repayment terms. He had agreed to pay back large sums of the loan after each harvest. The first big repayment was supposed to be due later that year. It was only early spring and harvest time was months away. But for some inexplicable reason, the bank was insisting that the first payment be made now. There was no way that Mr Davies could come up with the first payment now. He had put all his savings into the farm.

He had tried other banks, but they had not been willing to lend him any money. He had tried to explain that it was only for a few months. But it had been in vain.

Mr Davies had heard a rumour that there was some property developer interested in building on the land. He had even heard that somebody wanted to build a golf-course and country club. Mrs Tomms, the old woman that had sold him the farm had mentioned something about it. Apparently she had been offered a lot of money several times to sell out. But she had wanted the property to stay as a farm. Her husband had been a farmer all his life and loved working the land.

He couldn't understand the bank's attitude. Why were they changing the arrangements of the loan? Surely Mr Kerr would see sense and be reasonable. He was relying on it.

They hadn't long finished dinner when Mr Kerr arrived. David remembered seeing him before, when his dad was buying the farm. He had seemed nice enough then. David even remembered him talking to him about United.

Mr Davies and Mr Kerr disappeared into the sitting room. Mrs Davies flapped about getting tea and cakes sorted out. She was obviously anxious. David hadn't said anything to his sisters about what he had heard his mum and dad talking about. He didn't see any point. Sarah was in enough of a state as it was.

The two men seemed to be locked in the

room for ages. Occasionally David could hear his dad's voice raised, but he couldn't make out what was being said. It didn't sound as if it was going too well. David looked at the alarm clock in his room. Mr Kerr had been here for almost two hours. Eventually David heard the sitting room door open. He ran to the top of the stairs.

"I am sorry Mr Davies, that's the way it has to be," David heard the deep voice that he recognised as Mr Kerr's.

"We've been over this quite enough. I'm sorry I have to go. I've spent too much time on this already. Either get the money to the bank by close of business on Monday or lose the farm. That's our decision," Mr Kerr added sternly.

"But I still don't understand. What's caused you to change what we had agreed? If this is to do with that golf development, I'll take you lot to court," Mr Davies stated angrily.

"I'm sorry, I have to go. Do what you want, but if we don't see you on Monday, repossession papers will be served first thing Tuesday morning," Mr Kerr said as he went out the front door.

David heard his dad slam the front door shut.

Chapter 8

Mr Kerr rushed from the house, protecting himself from the heavy rain with his brief-case. He jumped into his car, a brand new white BMW. David watched him from his bedroom window. David was reluctant to go anywhere near his dad right now.

In the car, Mr Kerr struggled to keep his face straight. As soon as he had driven out of the farm gates on to the main road, a broad grin appeared on his face. He quickly dialled a number on the mobile phone to his side. After a couple of rings someone answered

"It's done. A few more days, and we're on our way. This is the big one Jim. We'll make a cool million from this deal," Mr Kerr spoke loudly, battling against the noise of the car.

"How did it go? No problems?" asked Jim Cullen, Kerr's business associate.

"No problem at all," replied Kerr. "He is just a small-time farmer. I had to spin it out of course. Pretend that we had tried to help him."

"Does he suspect anything?" Cullen asked, sounding a little less composed than his partner.

"Well, he has heard about the development. Threatened to take us to court. But he'll never be able to prove anything. I've covered all our tracks," replied Kerr

"I hope you have, mate. I really hope you have," Cullen stated nervously.

Chapter 8

"Don't worry, Jim. I've taken care of everything. Once we serve the papers on Tuesday we can celebrate. Until then, business is as normal. See you tomorrow. Bye."

Kerr pressed the end call button on the phone.

He looked in the rear view mirror and allowed himself another smile.

"You've made it now, son. You're in the big time," he thought as he looked at himself.

Kerr had been manager of the local bank for 5 years. He had worked up from a clerk position to run the bank. He had always been ambitious. To most, Kerr's career would have been considered a success. Not to Kerr. He thought he deserved better. He had been really irked when he was passed over twice for better jobs at the bank's headquarters. He hated being stuck out in a small rural town, pandering, as he saw it to a load of peasants.

Now he was using his position at the bank to cheat a family out of their home, their livelihood, to get what he wanted – money. He had already signed pre-contractual agreements with a major development company. His dream was going to be reality.

He smiled again.

The road ahead was very dark, but the new car's powerful headlights cast out a strong, wide, bright beam. Kerr lived on the other side of town, but the country roads were quiet and it wouldn't take him long to cover the few miles. As the car approached a sharp bend Kerr slowed down. He knew the road well. Just beyond the corner stood the old stone bridge spanning the river. As the BMW came round the bend, the car's headlights picked out some obstruction blocking the road over the bridge.

"What now?" exclaimed Kerr impatiently, under his breath. It was now raining very heavily and the last thing he wanted was to get out in the wet and struggle with some fallen tree or other. He could see now that it was a tree blocking the road. It didn't occur to Kerr that it was very strange for a tree to end up spanning a bridge, with water on either side.

Kerr stopped the car a couple of yards short of where the tree lay and switched the engine off. He stared out of his windscreen for a few moments, shook his head and then reached for his door handle. As he stepped out of the car, he immediately felt the rain pelting down on him. He cursed the weather. He walked up to the tree and stood over it. There was no way it seemed that he was going to be able to move it. He put his foot on top of the tree, testing if it could be rolled away. It wouldn't budge.

Suddenly, a loud noise came from behind him. Kerr immediately recognised the sound of his own car's high pitched revving. Someone had got into his car, switched the engine on and was revving the engine, pressing the accelerator up and down.

"What the Devil! What do you think you are playing at!?" Kerr shouted angrily, peering through the headlight's beam. He lifted his hand to his, eyes trying to block the glare and make out who was sitting behind the wheel of his car. The glare was strong and he could see nothing except what looked like a hat.

He started to move towards the car. But as he did, the car started to move towards him.

"Stop right there!!" Kerr shouted, his anger rising.

The car was only a few feet away now. It started to move more quickly. Kerr took a couple of steps back. He tried again to make out who was on the other side of the windscreen. He still couldn't see clearly. The lights blinding him. The car kept coming. His anger quickly turned to fear, as he sensed he was in real danger. The fear almost paralysing him to the spot.

Kerr made a move to his left, trying to get out of the car's path. But as he did, the car immediately turned and continued straight for him, slowly still, but quite deliberately. Kerr looked around. The tree was behind him to his right now. Its long branches blocking his way and impeding his retreat. To his left, the bridge wall. He edged a little more backwards. The car kept coming. There was only one way to go. He had to jump onto the wall. The bridge wall was very narrow, only about five inches wide. Kerr put his hand on top of the wall and leapt up. He wavered slightly, his arms flapping. His upper body leaned over, his eyes fixing on the water below. The heavy rain had turned the normal sleepy river into a raging torrent.

Kerr regained his balance and turned round.

"Right, this isn't funny any more!!" He shouted, trying to inject some form of authority into his wavering voice.

"Get out of my car!!" he screamed.

As if in reply to Kerr's demand, the car stopped, inches from the wall, and the car door started to open. Slowly the dark figure started to get out. Kerr narrowed his eyes, following the stranger's movements as it came round from behind the door.

Kerr stared hard, the effects of the lights' glare disappearing, the figure becoming clearer.

"Oh my God! What the. . .?!" the horror in his voice was chilling.

Kerr moved to step back, forgetting where he was. As he wavered, his feet struggled to regain grip. It was too late. He couldn't stop himself, he was going over. As he fell back he managed to grab hold of the wall with one hand. The skin tearing from his fingers as they tried to carry his full weight. His hand was slipping. He stretched out with the other hand trying to get another hold on the wall. He couldn't make it.

He looked at the rushing water below.

"Help. Help me please!" Kerr pleaded.

The pain in his fingers was too strong, the weight too much. He started to slip away. As his hand came away from the wall, and he began his deadly fall, he caught glimpse of a head leaning over the wall. A wooden head.

The noise of the wind and the rain drowned out his screams as he plunged into the rushing water.

The scarecrow turned away.

Chapter 9

The next morning, Saturday, the Davies'
house was sombre. Everyone could see that
Mr Davies was in a terrible mood. David had
heard his mother crying for most of the
night. Even now her eyes were red and sore
looking. David's were too. He had managed
to sleep very little over the past two nights
and he still hadn't been able to talk to his
dad. Mr Davies had stormed out minutes
after Mr Kerr had left and hadn't returned
until after everyone had gone to bed.

Sarah and Emma had no idea what was

going on, but David knew the family was in serious trouble. He had clearly heard Mr Kerr's ultimatum. His dad had to pay the bank by Monday or they were going to lose the farm.

David was glad it was Saturday. He couldn't have faced school again. His head was a mess. He was tired, confused, worried and scared.

His dad was messing about in the barn, repairing the digger. It had suddenly broken down first thing that morning as he had eventually started to clear the field in front. The field with the scarecrow in it.

David was waiting for his dad to come in. He had made up his mind that no matter what, he had to tell his dad about the scarecrow. Even if his dad refused to accept what he was saying, at least he would have got the thing off his chest. He felt so lonely and isolated. There was of course Sarah, but he needed his dad to know.

As David sat waiting, the phone rang. Sarah ran to answer it, expecting to hear her friend's voice. She was expecting a call. She was disappointed.

"Mum, it's that Constable Collins again," she shouted, trying to reach her mum upstairs.

Mrs Davies came down, the Morrison episode long replaced by the worries of the family's financial problems.

She took the receiver from Emma.

"Hello constable, how can I help you?" she asked

David moved into the hallway where his mother was taking the call. He watched as the shock appeared on her face. She put her hand over the receiver.

"David, go and fetch your dad, quickly," she ordered.

David could see the anxiety in her eyes, and spun round immediately running to get his dad.

The two returned quickly. Mrs Davies was standing by the telephone. Rooted to the spot since Constable Collins had hung up.

Mr Davies rushed to his wife's side, anticipating that her legs were about to give up on her. He ushered her into the sitting room.

Mrs Davies spoke first, "He was sitting on that chair a matter of hours ago."

"What is it, pet, what's happened now?" asked Mr Davies, puzzled and worried.

Mrs Davies related her brief conversation with Constable Collins. She explained that they had found Mr Kerr's car in the river this morning. He was missing but they feared the worst. The river had been so high last night, nobody could have survived the current. They were searching downstream for his body.

"But, how on earth? Where did this happen?" Interrupted Mr Davies.

Chapter 9

"Next to the old bridge, on the way to town. They reckon he committed suicide. They could find no evidence of the car losing control on the road. They think he just calmly drove up and drowned himself." Mrs Davies replied, her eyes filling up.

"Oh John! What's going on? First that madman the other night and now this. What's happening here?" Mrs Davies pleaded, beginning to break down.

Mr Davies held his wife in his arms, trying to comfort her. His mind drifted to the meeting he had held with Kerr the night before.

David had listened to his mum relating the news about Kerr. It didn't take him long to add the Kerr incident to all the others. Kerr was threatening the farm. David had heard the rumours, too, about the golf course development. Most of the town seemed to know that Kerr had wanted their farm for some time. Last night it had looked as though he was about to get his way with the Monday deadline. David didn't buy the suicide story. Something or somebody was to blame. David knew that the scarecrow had been at work again.

David waited for his dad to come out of the sitting room.

"Dad, I have to talk to you," David started.

"Is it important, son? I need to see to your mum. This business has really upset her," replied Mr Davies.

"Dad, before I tell you anything, I need you to come outside with me. I need you to look at the scarecrow with me," David continued

"Look, son enough of this nonsense," Mr Davies snapped.

"Dad, just do it, right!?" David insisted, raising his voice.

Mr Davies was taken aback by his son's tone. Normally, he would have given him a clip round the ear for such cheek. But he recognised that there was something upsetting David. He put his arm around him.

"Come on. Let's go then," Mr Davies said, heading for the kitchen door.

The two crossed the courtyard, in silence, climbed the fence and made their way across the field to where the scarecrow stood. David approached the wooden figure nervously. Mr Davies could see that his son was really bothered by the scarecrow David lifted the hat from the scarecrow's head and pointed to the words engraved on top.

Mr Davies was a good 18 inches taller than his son, and he could easily see the verse written on the bald head.

This land is yours for you to scare
All beings who perchance do dare
To disturb or threaten without pity
This house's peace and prosperity

The big farmer looked at his son and then

read the words over again, as if to make sure he understood their meaning.

"This is crazy. Surely this can't be," he said, shaking his head. "Let's go back."

They walked slowly back to the house. On the way, David rapidly ran through all the events of the past few days, connecting everything back to the words written on the scarecrow's head. In every case the person or animal affected had been connected to the farm and in some was threatening or disturbing it.

To disturb or threaten without pity
This house's peace and prosperity

David told his dad about Sarah and he witnessing the scarecrow disappearing and then reappearing.

When they reached the kitchen door, Mr Davies looked back. The scarecrow looked so normal. Like all the scarecrows he had seen in all the years he had been working as a farmer.

As they entered the kitchen, Mr Davies took his son's arm.

"Listen, son. Don't say a word of this to anyone. Especially not to your mother. She is at her wits' end at the moment. I'll have to think about this for a while. I don't want to make us the laughing stock of the whole town," he paused, his mind struggling to accept what seemed inconceivable.

But he was beginning to share his son's anxiousness. At least, he thought, if there was something going on it didn't seem to be posing any threat to his family. If it was the scarecrow, it seemed to be trying to protect them.

"I have to go into town now, to the bank," he continued, "and see how things stand for Monday. I don't know how this business with Mr Kerr is going to affect things. When I come back, we'll light a fire and burn the damn thing, and then let's see what happens."

Mr Davies left 10 minutes later. The bank was usually shut on Saturday's, but Mr Davies had managed to get someone on the phone. As the news had broken about their manager some of the staff had gone in to find out more.

David was worried. He had felt better telling his dad and he was happy to see that his dad seemed to share his concerns, however he wished that they had dealt with the scarecrow before he had left for town.

The hours passed slowly. David remained in his room until late afternoon. His dad had still not come back. He tried to keep his mind off things by playing his guitar and then some computer games. But his mind kept wandering to the scarecrow. Eventually he pulled back his curtains to have another look at the wooden man.

David stepped back. The fear returning

in a flash. The scarecrow had gone. He ran downstairs and scanned the courtyard from the kitchen door.

"Has Dad come back and taken the horrible thing off to burn it?" he thought, more in hope than anything. He ran out to see if he could see his dad's car or his dad himself. There was no sign. He heard a noise from the barn. He hesitated and then walked towards the entrance. Suddenly, from inside, he heard a voice.

"Looking for me, David?"

David froze. It was not his dad's voice. It was not any voice he recognised. He could sense the presence in the barn before he could see it. He entered the barn, his legs like jelly, the fear taking over his complete body.

"Hello, David," the wooden scarecrow stepped from behind some bales of hay, moving in a slow, deliberate manner.

David stood motionless, unable to speak.

All his fears were now reality. There was a wooden monster. Morrison had not been a madman. As far as he could tell this 'thing' in front of him was really dangerous.

The scarecrow's strained, slightly high-pitched voice, continued.

"David, do not stand in my way. I was made for this. I am doing what I must do."

David struggled to speak, his throat and lips completely dry. Eventually he blurted out, "But why, why?"

"I serve the farm, David. I was made to protect it. People are not important. People come and go, but the land remains forever. I serve the land. The farm and the land," the scarecrow replied.

The significance of the scarecrow's words hit David. The scarecrow wasn't protecting them, it was only interested in the farm, the land. Anything that threatened the land was in danger.

"Do not stand in my way, David. Do not

try to stop me. Heed my words," the scare-crow hissed.

He moved towards David. David closed his eyes, paralysed by fear. He felt the scare-crow brush past him. His legs wavered. He felt the scarecrow's presence disappear. David opened his eyes. He was alone. He fell to the floor, his legs finally giving way.

Chapter 10

"David! David!"

David opened his eyes. Sarah was standing above him.

"What's happened to you, David? Are you alright?" Sarah asked, a little shocked by the sight of her brother sprawled on the barn floor.

David picked himself up, his legs still a little unsteady and his head sore from hitting the barn floor. He had been unconscious for an hour or so. He immediately looked beyond his sister. In the field behind he could see the still, dark figure back in its usual spot.

"Come on, Sarah, let's get out of here," David stated, grabbing his sister's arm.

"Now!" he insisted, as his sister hesitated, staring out into the field, sensing the scarecrow was the reason for her brother's state.

They ran back to the kitchen. Mrs Davies was working at the sink. David and Sarah walked through the kitchen and upstairs.

"What is it, David? What is going on?" Sarah asked anxiously.

"We are in danger, Sarah. Real danger." David replied.

David told her about his encounter in the barn. Sarah buried her head in her pillow, her brother's words sending a chill right through her.

"Sarah, I want you to get Mum and take her into the sitting room and keep her there. Make up some story about school, keep her talking. Don't come out till I get back."

David instructed his sister.

"David, where are you going? What are you going to do?" Sarah pleaded, unsure what was going through her brother's mind.

David knew what he had to do. He couldn't afford to wait till his dad got home. He was going to have to do it himself. His family was in danger and he had no idea when the scarecrow was going to strike again, or against who. He was already getting worried that his dad had taken so long. Maybe the scarecrow would see his family as a threat. Maybe it would blame them if the farm were ripped up and turned into some golf-course or other.

"Go Sarah, get Mum!" David said, pacing the room, thinking his way through his next move.

David heard his mum and Sarah go into the sitting room. He ran downstairs, out the kitchen door and into the hut close by. He knew what he was looking for. He had seen it there the other day. Where was it now?

David moved his bike. There it was. David picked up the old oil lamp. He lifted the lid. Good, there was plenty of oil in the bottom. David ran back to the kitchen. It was getting dark now. David searched in the sink drawer. He found the box of matches and stuffed them into his pocket.

He ran to the barn and grabbed as much hay as he could carry. He stopped as he came out of the barn, and looked into the field. The scarecrow was still. David took a few deep breaths and walked forward. He climbed the fence, careful not to spill the oil from the lamp. As he approached the wooden monster, he had no idea what to expect. He kept his eyes fixed on it. It could have moved at any point. He had to take his chance. He had to protect his family.

He had no idea what governed when and how the scarecrow could come to life.

David came up to the scarecrow and

started wrapping the hay around the monster's legs. David didn't take his eyes off the scarecrow's face – no movement, thank God. He searched in his pocket. The matches weren't there. His blood rushed. Other pocket, idiot! He found them. He had to put the lamp down to light the match. The match lit first time. He put it to the wick, "Come on, come on," he pleaded, urging the wick to take light. The wick flickered and the flame took hold. He lifted the lamp above his head, preparing himself to smash it down with all his force at the base of the scarecrow. He hesitated. He could hear the sound of a car approaching.

David glanced round, hoping to see his dad's car, a sense of relief filling him. As he turned away, his eyes momentarily leaving the monster's face, he felt something grab the lamp. He spun round, the scarecrow's face was smiling, an evil smile. The scarecrow reached out, its hand tightening round

David's neck. David lashed out and ran. He could hear the scarecrow following behind, its legs speeding through overgrown grass. He could sense he was close. David clambered over the fence, as he had done the previous day when he had read the words on the scarecrow's head.

As he landed on the other side, the scarecrow landed too. The monster still held the oil lamp. The lamp's glow casting an eerie light across the scarecrow's face. The scarecrow moved round blocking David's path to the house.

David looked around, his desire for survival controlling his fear. He made to go right, stopped, and darted left making for the barn. He ran in and buried himself behind some bales of hay, the chickens flapping nervously at the noise of him rushing in. The scarecrow followed slowly, knowing he had his prey trapped.

David could see the light from the lamp's

glow lighting up the entrance as the scarecrow walked in. He crouched down, trying
to calm his breathing, trying to think what
to do next. He lifted his head slightly. His
eyes found a gap between two bales Peering through the bales, he could trace the
scarecrow's movements by the movements
of the light. He was coming closer.

The scarecrow's chilling voice broke the
silence.

"David, I warned you. Now you must
pay the price."

David looked up. The bales of hay were
piled three high. The scarecrow was directly
in front of him now, on the other side of the
bales. David took a couple of paces back and
steadied himself. The scarecrow spun round,
sensing David's movement. David ran,
jumped and launched himself at the bales
of hay. The stack wavered. The scarecrow
looked up just as the first bale hit him. The
oil lamp smashed to the floor, and burst into

flames. The scarecrow's legs and arms, stuffed with hay, immediately caught fire. Within seconds, the tinder dry bales all over the barn were in flames. The chickens scampered frantically trying to make their exit. Their noise adding to the chaotic scene.

David tried to pick himself off the floor, but the whole barn now seemed like one big ball of fire. He could just make out the spot where the scarecrow had been. He caught sight of something. He recognised the scarecrow's old hat. He couldn't see anything else except flames. He started to crawl forward, the smoke beginning to enter his lungs. His head started to sway. He started to cough, struggling for every breath. The heat was over-powering.

Suddenly he felt something reaching for him, pulling at his legs. He tried to kick free, crawl away, but the smoke had taken its toll and he had no strength. He could run no more. He felt himself being lifted in the air.

His heart was pounding. He was helpless.

"Come on, son. Let's get you out of here." Mr Davies threw his son over his shoulder and rushed out of the barn. He lay his son down at the kitchen door. David struggled to catch his breath, the smoke still deep inside his lungs. He felt his mum's arms around him, his head still swimming, his vision blurred. Mrs Davies hugged him tightly, shocked at her son's state.

Mr Davies knelt down in front of his son.

"Is it all over Davey? Is he gone?" Mr Davies asked, two hands on his son's shoulders.

David looked to the barn, the flames leaping high into the sky. He looked back at his dad and nodded his head.

"He's gone, Dad."

David stood up and took a few steps towards the barn. Mr Davies came and stood by his side. They stared at the wall of flames in front of them.

"The Farm is safe son. Kerr was the problem. He was crooked," Mr Davies said, his broad arm over his son's shoulder

"The scarecrow saw to Kerr, Dad. I am sure of it," David said, looking up at his father. "He wasn't interested in people, only the land and the farm."

"Well, he has protected it for the last time. It's up to us now," Mr Davies stated, reassuringly, turning back to the house. "Come on, son. Let's get you inside."

David looked out to the empty field, one last time. At last he felt safe.

Epilogue

"David, will you stop reading that paper and give me a hand," David's wife, Anne, snapped impatiently. "It was your idea to go for this picnic, so come on."

David put down the paper and helped his wife lay out the blanket on the grass. It was Sunday afternoon and it was a scorcher. As soon as David had woken up that morning and seen the blue sky, he had decided that it was a good day to pack the family in the car and travel to one of their favourite spots in the hills near there home. The kids loved to get out in the open and explore.

The journey had taken them about an hour and the two boys, Alan and Paul, had been in good spirits, despite the heat in the car. Alan had just turned five and Paul was almost three years old. They were very close and loved to play together.

Within minutes, Ann had covered the blanket in all sorts of delights: juice and cake for the boys, and sandwiches and a bottle of chilled wine for herself and David.

"Go and find the boys dear, it's all ready," Anne said, spotting her husband picking up the paper again.

The boys never wandered far. They were explorers, indeed, but they weren't that brave yet.

David had kept one eye on his sons, and seen them wander down a small path a few yards away. David followed the path for about ten to fifteen yards through the trees.

He soon heard the noise of the two boys playing. He spotted them half way up a wooden railed fence, pointing into the field straight ahead.

The scarecrow stood about twenty yards from the fence.

The boys heard their dad approach. They turned, broad smiles, lighting up their faces.

"What are scarecrows supposed to scare, Dad?" Alan asked, looking back at the scarecrow.

"Oh, they look after the crops, they just scare away anything that tries to eat the crops."

"So they're not supposed to scare us," little Paul asked, innocently.

David smiled, the memories buried deep inside him.

"No, son, they are not supposed to scare us. Come on let's go. Mum has some treats for you," he replied, lifting the two boys off the fence, one in each arm. He set them down and started to chase them up the path towards their afternoon feast.

As the boys ran on, David stopped. He couldn't resist a glance back. His body froze.

The field was empty.

We hope you enjoyed this story from the Creepers series. There are six titles for you to collect:

Ghost Writer

The Piano

Beggar Boy

The Scarecrow

Mirror Mirror

The Wishing Well

This series was conceived by Edgar J Hyde and much of the text was provided by his minions under slavish conditions and pain of death! Thankfully none of the minions defied their master and so we can say 'thank you' to them for toughing it out and making this series possible

Ghost Writer

Charlie is a 15-year-old, budding writer. When his family move to a large old house in the country he becomes the unsuspecting contact for a spirit writer who is trying to communicate with the living. How can the strange passages that appear overnight, in Charlie's own handwriting, be the work of anyone else but him? Who will believe his incredible story? The ghost seems to be trying to tell him of a dark secret and a cruel injustice. When Charlie starts to have a chilling recurring dream about his own death and he and his brother, Neil and sister, Kate start to see apparitions, they decide that they must investigate the ghost writer's secret - with terrifying consequences!

Mirror Mirror

When she and her family visit a local antique shop to buy a fabulous mirror, Sophie is tranfixed by a music box ballerina and insists that she must have it. Little do any of the family know of the dark and tragic history behind the mirror and the music box, and their link to the person who calls herself the Keeper of Lost Souls. Sophie and her sisters, Amy-Beth and Lucy , with the help of their unpredictable Aunty Patsy, must discover the true story of the girl in the mirror. They must free her from the terrifying past that the mirror has witnessed and makes her relive again and again.

The Piano

Roger and Emily Houston can't believe the bargain they have found when they buy a piano for a mere £200 - just perfect for the piano lessons of their children Victoria and Darryn. Their delight soon turns to amazement and horror - the piano has a life (or is that a death?) of it's own. The melodies that it plays over and over again are (literally) haunting and it becomes clear that someone from their past has a message for the Houston family about a very important decision they are about to make.

The Scarecrow

A horrific attack takes place on an isolated farm. A shivering, terrified man is found in shock, his tongue removed. The shock is too much for him and he kills himself leaving a note which claims that he was a burglar who was stopped from breaking into the farm by a scarecrow, who then ripped out his tongue. Of course no-one believes the note. But, David, who lives on the farm, knows that the noisy farmyard cockerel has been found throttled, his beloved dog has mysteriously gone missing and Jonesy a harmless local character has also been viciously silenced - they must be connected with the sightings of a scruffy, barely-human creature on the prowl. David decides he must solve the mystery himself but doesn't realise just what he is getting himself into.

The Wishing Well

Tom's family have moved to a farm in the country and he is very unhappy about the whole idea. To make matters worse his first day at his new school is as bad as he had at first dreaded and the imbecilic school bullies are soon after him. Tom finds sanctuary in a peaceful area of his family's new property that contains an old well. To his amazement and delight a heartfelt wish for revenge against his enemies spoken into the echoing depths of the well comes true. But Tom is about to find out that every malicious wish for revenge that is granted includes a sinister payback for the well's evil sprite occupant and soon the chaos she is creating seems uncontrollable. How can Tom stop her before she destroys everything and everyone in her path?

Mirror Mirror

When she and her family visit a local antique shop to buy a fabulous mirror, Sophie is tranfixed by a music box ballerina and insists that she must have it. Little do any of the family know of the dark and tragic history behind the mirror and the music box and their link to the person who calls herself the Keeper of Lost Souls. Sophie and her sisters, Amy-Beth and Lucy , with the help of their unpredictable Aunty Patsy, must discover the true story of the girl in the mirror. They must free her from the terrifying past that the mirror has witnessed and makes her relive again and again.

The Piano

Roger and Emily Houston can't believe the bargain they have found when they buy a piano for a mere £200 – just perfect for the piano lessons of their children Victoria and Darryn. Their delight soon turns to amazement and horror – the piano has a life (or is that a death?) of it's own. The melodies that it plays over and over again are (literally) haunting and it becomes clear that someone from their past has a message for the Houston family about a very important decision they are about to make.

Beggar Boy

Life isn't easy for Tommy and his mother. The most important things in life for the rest of the occupants of Montague Street are money and status symbols, and these are two things that Tommy and his mother definitely do not have. The shallow and cruel children of the street taunt Tommy by calling him 'beggar boy'. Just when he thinks he can stand no more of their petty jibes, a strange ragged boy comes to his defence. Tommy is appreciative but puzzled at the sudden appearance of his scruffy friend and at his new ally's amazing talent for creating fear and chaos in the lives of his affluent enemies. Where does the boy come from and, more puzzlingly, how can he appear and disappear so quickly?